Michael, 1997
Merry Christmas!
Have your Papa show
you the pictures in this
book. Someday I'll read
the story to you.
We love you!!

Aunt Debra +
Uncle George

# THE ADVENTURES OF
# SPACE GECKO

## BY BRUCE HALE

WORDS + PICTURES PUBLISHING, INC.

This book is dedicated to my wife, Janette.

Also by Bruce Hale:
Legend of the Laughing Gecko
Surf Gecko to the Rescue!

Library of Congress Catalog Card Number: 94-90355
ISBN: 0-9621280-2-3

Printed in Hong Kong.

O ne hot island day, Moki the Gecko argued with his parents because they wouldn't get him a new surf-board. "You're so mean!" he shouted, and stomped down to the beach to cool off. But when he returned, something was different. Something was wrong.

He looked all around. Nobody home. Moki went to the other animals asking, "Have you seen my parents?"

But nobody had. The little gecko dragged home alone.

Outside the door sat his friend, Pueo the owl.

"Pueo, I can't find my parents," sighed Moki. "I don't know what to do."

The owl shifted slowly from foot to foot. "You're not going to like this," he said. "'Io the Hawk saw the whole thing."

Moki braced himself: "What?"

Pueo continued, "Your parents were upset. They went walking on the side of the island where nobody goes, by the lake where Moon takes her bath. They got careless. Your parents fell in the moon water."

"No!" said Moki. He knew that if you touched moon water, you could go crazy, or even worse, you could be captured by the moon. Were his parents so upset they forgot this?

"Moon took them up into the sky," the owl said softly. "They're gone, Moki."

Moki flopped down and cried from his heart. Pueo brushed velvety wingfeathers over his friend's shoulders. "Oh, Moki, don't worry — we'll think of something," he said. "Come on, let's go see 'Io the Hawk. Maybe she can tell us more."

Moki and Pueo found the hawk perched on the old
ironwood tree.

"Hmph," she sniffed. "I've told you all.
Your careless parents took the fall,
and now you want to bring them back?
All I can say is, 'good luck, Jack.'"
'Io returned to grooming her
bright feathers.

"But 'Io, I must go help them,"
Moki replied. "Please, can you
fly me to the moon?"

The hawk looked icicles at
Moki with her golden eyes.
"Why should I try?"
she asked him. "See,
what have you ever done
for me?
You interrupt me
with your woe.
I've told you all I can,
now go!"

Moki slumped away. "Aw, don't worry," said Pueo. "She's just sore because she knows she can't fly as high as the moon. No bird can."

"But how will I ever get to my parents?" asked the little gecko. Pueo scratched his head. "There's one last chance, but it could be dangerous," he said. "Go ask the great volcano. If she doesn't burn you up, she just might help you. Good luck."

By the time Moki reached
the volcano, the afternoon
sun hung low. He took a deep
breath and started climbing.
Up he went, higher and higher.
Clouds brushed his face like the
fingers of ghosts, but still he
climbed on.

Once Moki slipped and hung
by his tail over a long drop. He
grabbed for a rock, but it fell off the
cliff. Would Moki follow? No -- his
sticky gecko feet helped get him back
on the trail.

Finally, he stood at the top. Hot steam poured from the mouth of the crater as he tiptoed nearer. Moki kneeled.

"Great Volcano, I bring an offering," he said, placing a special plant gently on the rock. "My parents fell in moon water and Moon took them away. Please help me save them."

The volcano hissed softly, "Why? They made their mistake. What's done is done."

"But it's my fault," said Moki. "I made them so angry, they got careless. Besides, I love them. I can't just let them go without doing something."

The volcano steamed in silence. "You want my help? Very well," she said at last. "Come closer." Moki walked to the jagged edge of the crater. The heat made him sweat like a waterfall.

"Ready?" asked the volcano. "Y-y-yes, your volcano-ship," said Moki. "Then jump," commanded the fiery goddess. Moki just stood there. Only a crazy gecko would jump into red-hot lava.

"Why do you wait? Do you want my help or not?" rumbled the volcano. Her lava bubbled angrily. "Jump!" she boomed. Moki took two steps back, hopped and jumped.....

......into the heart of the crater.

FAVOOOMM! A huge blast of steam shot out of the volcano's mouth, sweeping Moki ahead of it, up into the night sky. Faster and faster he flew, past the highest clouds, away from the familiar Earth and into space itself. Moki shut his eyes tightly.

When he opened them again, he found himself drifting in a cool sea of midnight blue. Stars sparkled bright above and below him. The sky glowed and pulsed. Then Moki turned around.

Looming near in the night sky, filling his
sight like a huge silver ball, was the moon.
So beautiful, so big — she took his breath away.
As Moki drifted closer, he thought he could
see a woman's face behind the silver light.

Moon smiled, "Hello, little one, what are you doing
so far from home?"

"It's about my parents," said Moki. "Please. They
didn't mean to touch your water, I'd like them to come
home now."

Moon's smile faded. "Ah, your mother and
father," she said. "Too late. They fell in my lake, and
now they're mine."

"Please," said Moki. "Can't I do something to change your mind?"

"There is something," said Moon, "but I doubt you can do it. The jealous Sun has stolen my mirror, and I cannot look upon my face. You are small and clever.

"Bring me the mirror and I will free your parents."

"But how do I get it?" asked Moki.

"That's your problem," said Moon. Just then, a friendly asteroid -- or space boulder -- the size of a small dog drifted towards Moki.

"Can you help me?" he asked the asteroid. It bobbed up and down eagerly. "Thank you. I think I'll call you Simon, if you don't mind."

The friendly space boulder nodded again.

Moki sat in one of the asteroid's small craters and hung on tightly as the little space boulder picked up speed. Soon, they rounded the Earth and saw it ahead, blinding and glorious in the sky — the Sun.

Here goes nothing, thought Moki.  If I fail, I'll
probably end up as Roast Gecko Au Gratin.
    As he drew nearer, Moki could hardly see, for the
bright light.  He scrunched down lower, trying to hide.
But it was no use.

"Who's there?" called Sun. "Who comes to see me in all my splendor?"

"Moki, a small gecko from Earth," said Moki, sitting up.

"Don't you think I'm beautiful?" said Sun. "No star in the universe has rays as glorious as mine. I'm a superstar, I am."

Moon is prettier, thought Moki. But of course, he didn't say that. Instead, he asked, "How do you know you're so beautiful? Have you ever seen yourself?"

"What?! Foolish earth creature!" bellowed the sun. "Everyone knows I'm hot stuff. But it's true I haven't seen myself. That's why I got this." He held up a small mirror.

"Great Sun, you cannot see your whole body," Moki
said. "Better throw me the mirror, so I can show you."
Now the sun was bright, but he wasn't too bright,
you see. He tossed the mirror to Moki, who let Simon
the asteroid drift a little further away. "How's this?"
asked the gecko, holding up the mirror.

If you've ever tried to look at the
sun, you know how it can hurt your eyes.
But the Sun didn't know that. Blinded by his own light,
he howled like a mad dog. Moki saw his chance.
   "Go, Simon!" he shouted, and VAZZOOSH! -- the
asteroid zipped away from the Sun like a stone from a
slingshot.

"Come back here!" bellowed the Sun. His mighty rays shot out as Moki tried to shrink down into a crater. Too late! Fingers of flame burned Moki's tail. "Yow!" cried the gecko.

In another two shakes, the little asteroid flew beyond the sun's reach. Moki's poor tail was black, burnt and oh, so painful. It hurt worse than a thousand sunburns.

"I hope Sun learned his lesson," he told Simon. "I sure learned mine -- don't bug a superstar, or you might get burned."

Soon the asteroid brought him back to the moon.
Moon smiled hopefully, "Well? What luck?"
Moki managed to stand up. "I got your mirror," he
said. "Now give me back my parents."

Moon's smile melted like snow. "Not so fast," she said. "Maybe I have another task for you before I'll let them go."

Moki's shoulders sagged. Then, he slowly straightened and held up the mirror. "Maybe I'll take this back to Earth with me and neither one of us will get what we want," he said.

Moon sighed, "Oh, well. It was worth a try. Here, take my magic silver cup and pour this on your tail."

Moki poured the shining water on his blackened stump of a tail and — miracle of miracles — he grew back a brand new tail, strong and shiny and green. He tossed the mirror to the moon.

"I grant you a special gift," said Moon. "From now on, all geckos can grow back their tails as you have done. Now go around to my dark side where you will find your mother and father. Take them and return home, with my blessing."

Sure enough, on the Moon's dark side, Moki found his parents. They were having a party with some strange-looking space aliens.

The three geckos greeted each other with laughter and tears and "Oh-how-I-missed-you." Then, "I've come to take you home," said Moki.

"That's very brave of you to come this far," said his mother, "but we don't want to go."

"What?!" Moki the Gecko couldn't believe his ears.

"That's right," his father said. "We like it here with our new friends. Stay with us and become a moon gecko."

Moki looked up in the sky to see the Earth, floating like a blue-green ball. He looked at the moon -- no waves, no trees. Then he searched his heart.

"My home is back there," he said finally, "with the ocean and forest and volcano. I have to go, but how can I leave you here?"

Moki's mother stroked his face. "There comes a time of letting go," she said. "You're old enough to take care of yourself now. You've proved that."

Moki knew she spoke the truth.

"We'll miss you, but don't be a stranger," said Moki's father. "You know the way. Come visit us on your asteroid anytime you want to."

Moki hugged his parents tightly and wished them farewell. Even the aliens shed a tear or two as the brave gecko pointed his asteroid towards Earth and took off.

Simon the space boulder danced through the midnight blue sky, moving faster and faster as it neared the Earth. Before long, he and Moki ripped through the atmosphere and down through the high clouds.

Finally, they landed —KERBLUNK! — right in the ocean off Moki's beach. A gentle wave rolled the asteroid up the sand, tumbling the gecko in the surf.

    Standing on the sand, he looked up at the early
morning sky, lightening now.  The sadder-but-wiser
Sun waited just over the horizon.  The other way, low
above the island, Moon was sinking into bed.
    Moki thought he could see the faint outline of two
geckos crawling across her shining silver face.
    Goodnight, Mom and Dad, goodnight, Moon, he
smiled back.  And on the beach, the little asteroid rolled
in the surf, happy in its new home.